FELICITY'S NEW SISTER

FELICITY · 1774

BY VALERIE TRIPP

ILLUSTRATIONS DAN ANDREASEN

VIGNETTES SUSAN MCALILEY

THE AMERICAN GIRLS COLLECTION®

Published by Pleasant Company Publications
Previously published in *American Girl®* magazine
© Copyright 1999 by Pleasant Company
For information, address: Book Editor, Pleasant Company Publications,
8400 Fairway Place, P.O. Box 620998, Middleton, WI 53562.

Printed in Hong Kong.
99 00 01 02 03 04 05 06 C&C 10 9 8 7 6 5

The American Girls Collection®, Felicity®, and Felicity Merriman®
are trademarks of Pleasant Company.

Edited by Nancy Holyoke and Michelle Jones
Art Directed by Kym Abrams and Laura Moberly
Designed by Laura Moberly

Library of Congress Cataloging-in-Publication Data

Tripp, Valerie, 1951-
Felicity's new sister / by Valerie Tripp;
illustrations, Dan Andreasen; vignettes, Susan McAliley.—1st ed.
p. cm. — (The American girls collection)
Summary: Although she is tired of the responsibility of being the oldest sister,
Felicity realizes how much her family means to her when a
carriage accident puts her pregnant mother in danger. Includes a section on babies in
the late 1700s.

ISBN 1-56247-762-5
[1. Brothers and sisters—Fiction. 2. Babies—Fiction.]
I. Andreasen, Dan, ill. II.Title. III. Series.
PZ7.T7363Fekm 1999 [Fic]—dc21 98-34558 CIP AC

The
AMERICAN GIRLS
COLLECTION™

OTHER AMERICAN GIRLS
SHORT STORIES:

A REWARD FOR JOSEFINA

KIRSTEN ON THE TRAIL

HIGH HOPES FOR ADDY

SAMANTHA'S WINTER PARTY

MOLLY TAKES FLIGHT

PICTURE CREDITS

The following individuals and organizations have generously given
permission to reprint illustrations contained in "Looking Back":
p. 30—Colonial Williamsburg Foundation; p. 31—The Newark Museum/Art
Resource, NY; p. 32—Manchester City Art Galleries; p. 33—The Opie Collection;
p. 34—Colonial Williamsburg Foundation; p. 35—Pincushion courtesy of Six-Sept,
New York, an English Collectibles company; p. 36—York Castle Museum;
p. 37—Colonial Williamsburg Foundation; p. 38—Colonial Williamsburg Foundation;
p. 39—Litchfield Historical Society; p. 40—Photography by Jamie Young.

TABLE OF CONTENTS

FELICITY'S FAMILY

FATHER
*Felicity's father, who owns
one of the general stores
in Williamsburg.*

MOTHER
*Felicity's mother, who
takes care of her family
with love and pride.*

FELICITY
*A spunky, spritely
colonial girl, growing
up just before the
American Revolution.*

NAN
*Felicity's sweet and
sensible sister, who is
seven years old.*

WILLIAM
*Felicity's three-year-old
brother, who likes mischief
and mud puddles.*

POLLY
*Felicity's baby sister,
the newest Merriman,
who is born in
December 1775.*

MRS. WENTWORTH
*A lady who has
strong opinions.*

FELICITY'S NEW SISTER

Felicity Merriman closed the back door and tiptoed across the porch. She stood at the top of the steps for a moment. The December sky was wide and peaceful. The air was sharp and cold. It was a beautiful morning, and Felicity knew exactly how she wanted to start the day. She was going for a ride on her horse, Penny.

Felicity took a joyful leap off the porch and set off at a run to the stable. *Penny will go faster than ever before,*

"Where do you think you're going, Miss Felicity?"

thought Felicity. *I'll*—

"Where do you think you're going, Miss Felicity?"

I'm caught, thought Felicity unhappily. She stopped and turned around.

Rose, the Merriman family's cook, was standing in the doorway, her arms folded across her chest. "Your mother's having a breakfast party this morning, and she expects you to be there," Rose said.

Felicity frowned. "Oh, Rose," she began.

But Rose was firm. "Go inside and put on some better clothes," she said.

Felicity sighed and trudged slowly back toward the house.

"I know you'd rather gallop off on that horse you love," Rose said kindly. "But your mother needs your help now, and she'll need it even more after the baby's born. Being the eldest sister is a responsibility you can't run away from." She smiled at Felicity. "Don't look so cross. I have a nice tart for your breakfast."

Even the thought of one of Rose's tarts did not cheer Felicity as she went to her chamber to change. She was so tired of being indoors! Mother was expecting a baby. She needed Felicity's help in the house because she could not move very easily. When Mother wanted to rest, Felicity had to keep her sister Nan and

4

her brother William quiet. There was little time for her to ride or to play out of doors.

When holiday callers came, Felicity had to pour the tea, serve the cakes, and help keep the conversation going. Felicity felt as though she had been cooped up inside all December, listening to guests drone on about who had recently died, or married, or had babies.

Babies! Felicity thought sourly as she pulled on her petticoat. *Mother's new baby has made it a dull winter for me. And after the baby is born, I will have to help take care of it. I wish I were* not *the eldest sister in this family!*

Felicity went downstairs feeling very

sorry for herself. Her spirits dropped with every step, and they sank into her shoes when she saw who the breakfast guest was. Mrs. Wentworth! The most talkative lady in all Virginia!

Mrs. Merriman, Nan, and William were already seated at the dining table and Rose was serving the tarts when Felicity entered and made her curtsy. Mrs. Wentworth nodded to her but never stopped talking.

"Martha, you must do as I say," she was telling Mrs. Merriman. "You need a rest. You should go to your father's plantation. I'm going home Thursday. You and the children must ride to your father's plantation with me. Your

Rose was serving the tarts when Felicity entered
and made her curtsy.

husband can come down later."

"Oh, Mother!" exclaimed Felicity. "Can we go to Grandfather's? It would be so lovely!" Felicity imagined galloping across the frosty fields and tramping through the wintry woods. There were many servants at Grandfather's plantation. Felicity would not have to look after Nan and William, or help Mother. She would have no responsibilities at all!

Before Mother could answer, Rose rattled the plates. Mother looked up at her, and Felicity did, too. Rose did not say anything, but her feelings were clear from the expression on her face. She looked disapproving.

Mother spoke to Mrs. Wentworth.

"For days now, Rose has been telling me that the baby will come much sooner than we expect it," Mother said. "I am sure Rose does not think I should go far from home." She turned to Rose and asked, "Do you, Rose?"

"No, ma'am," said Rose firmly.

Felicity felt a flash of anger at Rose. She was glad Mrs. Wentworth spoke up quickly to say, "Now, Martha. The midwife says the baby won't come soon. I hardly think Rose knows more about babies than she does."

"Rose has been with me since before Felicity was born," said Mrs. Merriman. "She knows a good deal about babies. I suppose—"

Felicity could not contain herself a moment longer. "Oh, Mother," she burst out. "Please say we can go. Please. This is our last chance for fun before . . ."

Mrs. Merriman smiled. "Very well," she said. "We'll go. I have been feeling guilty about how little time you've had for yourself, Felicity. And you'll have even less after the baby is born. 'Twill do us all good to have a change."

Rose sighed. But the children cheered, and Mrs. Wentworth said, "It's settled then. My carriage will be here bright and early Thursday morning, and we'll be off!"

It was neither bright nor early Thursday when Mrs. Wentworth's carriage arrived. The luggage was loaded on quickly. Rose sat outside next to the driver, Caleb, and tucked her small bag under the seat. Everyone else sat inside, and the carriage set forth under a rainy afternoon sky.

The air was stuffy in the carriage. Nan and William were soon half asleep, lulled by the drowsy whispers of sleet and rain on the windows. Mrs. Wentworth talked on and on and on. Once in a while, Mother murmured politely, "Indeed!" With every jounce of the carriage, Felicity was jabbed by

Mrs. Wentworth's elbow, which felt remarkably sharp for one belonging to such a stout lady.

Felicity was impatient to get to Grandfather's plantation. She looked out the window at the dreary view as the carriage rolled along mile after mile.

The muddy road wound its way past bare black trees, empty brown fields, and gray stone walls. About ten miles outside Williamsburg, just past a deserted house, the road dipped into a gully that the rain had turned into a stream. As the carriage drove down into the gully, the wheels slipped on the muddy bank. *Thunk!* The carriage lurched, then slammed to a stop so violently that they were all thrown on top of one another.

"Help! Caleb!" shrieked Mrs. Wentworth. Nan and William cried out with fright.

Felicity heard a sickening *crack!* She looked down and gasped in fear. The floor of the carriage had split, and she could see water seeping through. The carriage was tilting so far to one side, it seemed as if it was about to topple over into the water.

Mrs. Wentworth shrieked again. "Caleb! What's happened? Get us out of here!"

Caleb and Rose sloshed through the water to the door of the carriage. Caleb wrenched the door open and leaned into the carriage. "We've crashed into the bank, ma'am," he said. "The undercarriage is cracked and the horse is lamed."

"Quick," said Rose. "Come out of the carriage before it falls on its side!"

"We must help Mrs. Merriman out first," said Mrs. Wentworth.

She supported Mother from behind, and Caleb held Mother's hands as she slid out of the carriage. Then Caleb helped Mother, and Rose helped Mrs. Wentworth through the water and up the bank.

"Make haste, children," Rose called.

But Nan and William shrank back into the dark carriage, looking terrified.

"Miss Felicity!" Rose shouted urgently.

"Nan and William are scared. You'd better go first so you can help them." When Felicity hesitated Rose said, "Hurry now! The water is getting higher."

Felicity wanted to cry out, "I'm scared, too!" But when she looked at Nan's and William's frightened faces, she felt sorry for them. *They're too scared to move, poor things,* she thought. *Rose is right. I'll have to go first.*

Pretending more courage than she felt, Felicity pushed herself through the door. She almost fell to her knees as the icy water curled around her feet and legs.

When she had her footing, Felicity turned back and held her arms open to William.

"Come on, William," she said as calmly as she could. "I'll catch you." William slid into her arms, and Felicity held him close.

"Now it's your turn, Nan," she said. "Don't be afraid. See? The water comes only to my ankles. 'Tis not deep at all."

Nan inched her way out of the carriage. "Oh, the water's cold!" she wailed when she stood in the stream.

"Aye," said Felicity. "Let's get out of it." Nan hurried out of the water. Felicity followed, carrying William, who clutched her tightly.

Caleb led everyone to the deserted house just above the gully. Inside the house it was as cold and dark as outside

*"Now it's your turn, Nan," Felicity said. "Don't be afraid. See?
The water comes only to my ankles. 'Tis not deep at all."*

in the winter twilight. But it was dry, and Caleb quickly started a fire. They all crowded near it, shivering, wet, and cold. By the fire's flickering light, Felicity saw that Mother looked pale.

Mrs. Wentworth straightened her hat. "Caleb," she ordered, "you walk back toward Williamsburg and get help. We'll wait here. Make haste. I'm quite uncomfortable in these wet clothes."

"Yes, ma'am," said Caleb. "I'll be back as soon as I can."

After Caleb left, Rose added some logs to the fire. Felicity took off her cloak and hung it up to dry. Suddenly, Mother gasped and held her hand to her side.

Rose rushed to her. "I think . . . I think the baby is coming," whispered Mother.

Oh no! thought Felicity.

"Nonsense," said Mrs. Wentworth briskly as she twisted the water out of her petticoats.

Mother was quiet for a moment. Then she gasped again and bit her lip.

Mrs. Wentworth looked alarmed. "Martha, do be sensible," she said. "You mustn't have that baby now. Wait."

"Mrs. Wentworth, ma'am, babies don't wait," said Rose. Gently, she helped Mrs. Merriman stand and go into the next room. "We'd better get ready to do all we can."

"Gracious me!" exclaimed Mrs. Wentworth. "I don't know the first thing

about babies!" But she followed Rose and
Mrs. Merriman.

Felicity was so frightened she was
trembling. *Mother and the baby are in
danger, and it's all my fault!* she thought.
If only I had not begged Mother to come!

At that moment, William's small
hand slid into hers. "Lissie," he whispered. "Is Mother having her new baby?"
His face was white.

Felicity remembered Rose saying,
"Being the eldest sister is a responsibility
you can't run away from." She took a
shaky breath and squeezed William's
hand. "Don't worry, William," she said.
"Rose will take care of Mother. And I will
take care of you and Nan. We will all be

fine." How she hoped that would be true!

Felicity made Nan and William comfortable in a corner by the fire. She took off their wet shoes and stockings and rubbed their feet dry. She sang to them softly, to cover the sound when Mother moaned or called out in pain.

For a while, all was quiet in the other room. Nan and William fell asleep. Felicity was too frightened to sleep. She sat absolutely silent, straining to hear, but not a sound came from the other room. She was wide awake when Rose came out and motioned to her. Carefully, so she wouldn't wake Nan and William, Felicity stood and went to Rose.

"Miss Felicity," said Rose. "I'm going to ask you to do a hard thing. Will you go back to the carriage and get my bag? I've got some things in it to help your mother. I'd go myself, but—"

"No, Rose!" said Felicity, pulling on her cloak. "I'll go!"

Rose nodded. "You're a brave girl. Hurry!" she said.

The rain was so cold it seemed to cut Felicity's face. She headed back to the gully, walking as quickly as she could on the slick ground. The bank of the gully was so slippery, Felicity slid down it on her bottom. She waded through the water to the carriage and found Rose's bag still under the driver's seat. It was soaking wet but unharmed. Felicity held the bag to her chest with both hands and stumbled back through the inky darkness to the deserted house.

Rose was waiting for her just inside the door. She took the bag and disappeared into the other room.

Suddenly, Felicity heard Mother cry out. Rose spoke, low and calm, soothing Mother and encouraging her. Mrs. Wentworth spoke, too. "Steady, Martha!" she said. "Steady!"

Then Felicity heard a mewing sound, like a kitten crying for milk. The mewing grew louder and stronger, till it was a good strong wail.

The baby! thought Felicity. She crept to the door and looked into the room. There was no fire, and just one candle, so the room was dark and shadowy. Mother looked up from the bed Rose had made on the floor and smiled at Felicity.

"Come in, Lissie," she said. "Come and see your new sister."

Felicity's legs felt weak as she walked over to Mother. She knelt on the floor next to her and peered down at the face in the bundle Rose was holding. *My baby sister,* she thought. Her heart was full of pride and love. *My new baby sister.*

She felt a hand on her shoulder.

"Come in, Lissie," Mother said. "Come and see your new sister."

Felicity hardly recognized Mrs.
Wentworth's voice, it was so shaky.

"Well, I'm an old fool," Mrs.
Wentworth said. "But I'm not such a fool
that I can't admit when I've been wrong.
Rose did know more than the midwife.
She was right about when the baby
would be born. And I'm not fool enough
to think I could have brought this babe
into the world without her help. Thank
God you were here, Rose."

"Yes, ma'am," said Rose. Then she
smiled at Felicity and said, "Everybody's
got to help when a baby comes, whatever
way they can."

Felicity smiled back proudly.

Gently and carefully, Rose handed

the baby to Felicity. "Your sister's a pretty little thing, isn't she, Miss Felicity, for all she was almost born in a stream like a polly-wog!" said Rose.

"We should name her Polly," said Felicity, "short for pollywog."

"Polly it is," said Mrs. Merriman. "That way we'll never forget the night she was born."

"Oh, I'll never forget this night!" exclaimed Felicity, looking at the baby's round, red face. "This is the night I became a sister all over again."

VALERIE TRIPP

Suzie, Rosemary, Kate, Granger, and Valerie Tripp

My sisters and I were very excited when our brother, Granger, was born. He arrived before Christmas and was the best present any of us could have imagined. We were pleased to become sisters all over again.

Valerie Tripp has written twenty-one books in The American Girls Collection, including six about Felicity.

A Peek Into
the Past

BABIES IN 1774

In colonial times, babies were born at home. The birth was usually attended by

This colonial midwife is showing the new baby to the father.

a midwife, who helped mothers during childbirth. Sometimes female relatives and servants were there also. After a baby was born, a woman like Felicity's mother stayed in bed for a week or more. She rested for up to a month to get her strength back. Slave women and other working mothers usually could not rest for so long. They needed to start working again as soon as they were able to.

A few weeks after the birth, babies were *christened*. Christenings were religious ceremonies attended by relatives and close friends. Parents often named their babies at christenings. Colonial parents chose names that had important meanings. They

In colonial times, birth certificates were works of art.

31

wanted their baby's name to reflect a virtue, such as Patience, Charity, or Prudence. Other names like Anne (which means "gracious"), Elizabeth (which means "oath of God"), and Katherine (which means "purity") were also popular in colonial times.

Godparents were chosen at the christening. Parents often chose one of their brothers or sisters or a close family friend. If the child's parents died, the godparents

This christening gown is made of ivory satin trimmed with silk braid and ribbons.

would be responsible for taking care of the child.

When a baby was born, the family celebrated with lots of food. They made a big *groaning cake* to celebrate the birth and served pieces to visitors. During the first few weeks and months after a baby's birth, the new mother also invited all her women friends to a *groaning party* to feast on a dinner of rich meats, pies, and tarts. Visitors often brought gifts of money, clothing, or pretty trinkets for the new baby.

This baby rattle has a whistle and bells for entertainment and a coral handle for teething.

Pincushions were also hung on the front door to announce the new arrival.

A popular baby gift in colonial times was a pincushion. Friends and relatives made pincushions in heart, star, ball, and square pillow shapes. Then they stuck straight pins in the cushions to form a design or verse. "Welcome Little Stranger" was the most common verse. Others were "Welcome as the Summer Flowers," or "Father's hope and mother's joy, welcome either girl or boy." The messages were usually careful not to say if the pincushion was for a girl or boy, since there was no way to predict which it would be!

Pins were a useful gift because mothers fastened baby diapers and clothes with them. During the Revolution, pins were scarce because they had to be imported from Europe. Safety pins didn't become common until the late 1800s. They must have been a relief. At least one mother wondered

Pincushions were usually made of white satin and often had a border of lace.

whether her baby was crying from "pains or pins"!

Colonial babies born before the 1760s were *swaddled*, or wrapped in long strips of cloth. People believed swaddling straightened babies' bones.

By the time Polly was born, people realized it could be dangerous for a baby to be tightly wrapped. So they loosened up!

A baby's very first bath was with warm water. Each bath after that got colder and colder until the baby was bathed

When a baby wore this swaddling set, only her arms were free to move.

only in cold water. Parents thought this would make their babies strong.

Babies like Polly learned to walk by standing in the center of *walking stools*. The stools often had a shelf for toys. As babies grew, they wore clothes that had *leading strings*. Leading strings were ribbons or cords fastened to the back of a dress or shirt. Parents held the

A colonial walking stool

strings to guide the child's steps and protect her from falls. When colonial babies started walking, they wore padded *pudding caps* to protect their

This pudding cap has lots of padding.

heads. Today some adults still call babies "puddin' heads"!

Babies like Polly were also laced into tiny corsets called *stays*. Parents thought stays gave their children good posture. As both boys and girls grew older, they wore dresses called *frocks*. By the time they were five or six, girls began dressing more like their mothers and boys were *breeched*. Breeching meant that boys began to dress like their fathers by wearing pants called *knee breeches*. From that time on, fathers took a greater role in teaching their sons,

38

while girls continued to follow their mothers' example.

The child sitting on the floor is a boy. He is only three years old—not old enough to wear breeches yet!

MAKE A COLONIAL BABY GIFT

Celebrate a new arrival.

Felicity loved becoming a big sister again. When she and her family arrived home with the new baby, there would have been many visitors to see Polly. Some of them might have brought a pincushion with them as a baby gift. Make a pincushion to celebrate a new baby in your home or in a friend's home.

YOU WILL NEED:

*2 pieces of solid-colored fabric,
each 5 by 5 inches*

Ruler

Fabric pen with disappearing ink

Embroidery hoop, 4 inches wide

Embroidery floss of different colors

Scissors

Embroidery needle

Straight pins

Sewing needle

Thread

Cotton balls

Tassels or cord, optional

1. Lay 1 piece of fabric on a table, with the *right side,* or front side, of the fabric facing up. Use the ruler and fabric pen to draw a line on the fabric 1/4 inch from each edge.

2. In the center of the fabric, write "Welcome Little Stranger" or the name of the baby and the year. If you make a mistake, wait a few hours for the ink to disappear, then try again.

3. Place the fabric in the embroidery hoop. Cut an 18-inch piece of embroidery floss. Separate 2 strands, and thread the needle. Tie a double knot near the other end of the floss.

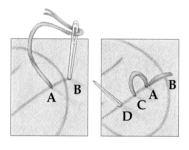

4. Backstitch your design. To backstitch, come up at A and go down at B. Come up at C and go down at A. Come up at D, and so on. Keep stitching!

5. When you near the end of your thread, tie a knot under the fabric close to your last stitch. Cut off the extra thread.

6. When you finish stitching, remove the embroidery hoop. Then lay the fabric pieces on top of each other, right sides together. Pin 3 edges together. Use the sewing needle and thread to backstitch the 3 sides, 1/4 inch from each edge.

7. Unpin the fabric and turn it right-side out. Stuff the pincushion with cotton balls until it's plump.

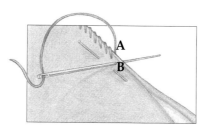

8. Tuck the raw edges of fabric inside the pincushion. Pin the edges together and sew the fourth side closed with a whipstitch. Bring the needle up at A, and then pull the thread over the fabric edge to go down at B. When you're finished, tie a knot and remove the pins.

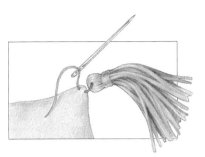

9. To decorate the outside of your pincushion, sew tassels to the corners. Or
   sew on a colorful cord for hanging.

THE AMERICAN GIRLS COLLECTION®

To learn more about The American Girls Collection, fill out the postcard below and mail it to American Girl, or call **1-800-845-0005**. We'll send you a free catalogue full of books, dolls, dresses, and other delights for girls.

I'm an American girl who loves to get mail. Please send me a catalogue of The American Girls Collection:

My name is _____

My address is _____

City _____ State _____ Zip _____

My birth date is $\frac{}{\text{Month}}$ / $\frac{}{\text{Day}}$ / $\frac{}{\text{Year}}$ 1961

And send a catalogue to my friend:

My friend's name is _____

Address _____

City _____ State _____ Zip _____

                                                                        1225